New Neighbors

"This is our son Eugene Spencer," said Mrs. Eastman.

Nora was stunned into silence. Gene was a boy. She could not believe it, and yet there he was standing right in front of her.

Nora stood looking at this new boy. She remembered that his mother said he was eight years old. She herself had been seven for only a short while and was going to remain seven for quite a long time. When she was playing with Teddy and Russell, seven seemed very old and important. But suddenly seven didn't seem very old. This was not the way Nora had imagined things at all.

Read all the books about
Nora, Teddy, Russell, and Elisa

Johanna Hurwitz

New
Neighbors
for Nora

illustrated by
Debbie Tilley

SCHOLASTIC INC.
New York Toronto London Auckland Sydney
Mexico City New Delhi Hong Kong Buenos Aires

ISBN 0-439-41974-3

Text copyright © 1979 by Johanna Hurwitz. Illustrations copyright © 2001 by Debbie Tilley. All rights reserved. Published by Scholastic Inc., 557 Broadway, New York, NY 10012, by arrangement with HarperCollins Publishers. SCHOLASTIC and associated logos are trademarks and/or registered trademarks of Scholastic Inc.

12 11 10 9 8 7 6 5 4 3 2 1   2 3 4 5 6 7/0

Printed in the U.S.A.   40

First Scholastic printing, December 2002

For my aunts
Cluck, Birdie, Al, Emmy, Dos,
Gin, and Totsie.
And, of course, my uncles too.

Contents

A New Neighbor

Sometimes Nora wished that everyone she knew lived in her apartment building. It would be fun if all her school friends and Grandma and Grandpa and Aunt Suzanne and the cousins all lived in the same apartment building. She would spend all her time going up and down in the elevator visiting them.

Since they didn't, Nora had made friends with most of the 200 people who did live in her building. If only there were more children, she thought.

Except for Nora, who was seven, and her little brother Teddy, who was five, the only other child in the whole building was Russell. He lived on the second floor and was four years old.

Despite their different ages, the three children were good friends. Living in the same building meant that even when the weather was bad or Mommy and Daddy were too busy to take them outside, they could play together.

One day Nora noticed that Russell's mother, Mrs. Michaels, was getting very fat. She saw a button pop off Mrs. Michaels' blouse when she and Teddy were having lunch in Russell's apartment. She had been taught that it was not polite to comment on such things, so she didn't say anything at the time.

But later, when she was back in her own apartment, she said to her mother, "Mrs. Michaels is getting awfully fat."

"You're right," said Mommy. "But she isn't really fat. She is growing a baby inside her. Soon Russell will have a new brother or sister."

"I hope it's a sister!" said Nora, delighted by the revelation.

"No, no," said Teddy. "I hope it's a brother."

"It will be a sister because I said it first," claimed Nora. "And besides, we already have two boys in our building and only one girl. If Russell gets a sister, there will be two girls and two boys."

Mommy laughed.

"Nobody will know till the new baby is born, and that won't be until next month."

The next several days the children thought about possible names for the new baby. They called out suggestions whenever they thought of them, as if they were guessing the secret identity of Rumpelstiltskin.

"How about Snow White, because there is snow on the ground?" offered Nora.

"That snow is dirty," said Teddy, looking out the window. "The baby should be named George Washington, because that is a famous name."

Now that she knew about the baby growing inside Mrs. Michaels, Nora was terribly impatient for it to come out. A month seemed a long time to wait for a baby. It was like waiting for your birthday, and, as Mommy pointed out, it was exactly that: waiting for a birth day.

One Sunday morning Nora and Teddy woke up to discover that there was a strange bundle of blankets in the middle of their bedroom floor.

A small head was poking from it.

"Russell! You came to play early," shouted Teddy with delight. This was a wonderful surprise.

Russell woke rubbing his eyes. He seemed surprised too, just as surprised as Nora and Teddy.

Then the bedroom door opened. It was Mommy, with a big smile on her face. She

hugged Russell and asked him, "Do you remember when your daddy brought you here in the middle of the night?"

"Where is my mommy?" asked Russell. He looked as if he was deciding whether or not he should cry.

"She is at the hospital with your daddy, and they will phone us as soon as the baby is born." Mommy smiled at Russell. "How would you like to help me make pancakes for breakfast?"

After breakfast, Russell was restless. He moved from the building blocks to the farm animals to the Play-Doh after just a couple of minutes at each. He kept running to the door to hear if his mother was coming. Nora and Teddy did their best to amuse him, but he did not want to play. Mommy said she would read a story to them. She was only on the second page when the telephone rang.

It was Russell's father with the exciting news: Russell had a baby sister named Elisa. Even Teddy rejoiced, though the baby wasn't a boy.

"Russell," said Nora, "we must go tell everyone!" Mommy agreed. So, carried away by Nora's excitement and determination to spread the news to all their neighbors, Teddy and Russell followed her.

First they went to Anita, who lived next door.

"Guess what!" demanded Nora when the door opened to their ring. And then before Anita could make even one guess, Nora said, "Russell has a new sister named Elisa." Anita smiled sleepily and congratulated Russell.

The children said good-bye and took the elevator up to the eighth floor. They rang the bell of Mrs. Wurmbrand. She was over eighty-five years old and walked slowly, so they had to wait a couple of minutes till she came to the door.

"Guess what!" said Nora.

"Is it trick or treat time again?" said their old friend, smiling.

"No!" Nora laughed. "Russell has a baby sister. She's a girl named Elisa."

"What lovely news and what a beautiful name!" said Mrs. Wurmbrand. "Don't go away," she instructed the children, and she went back into her apartment. When she returned she was holding three chocolate bars.

"This is for the celebration of such a

wonderful event," she said. "But I think you should save them till after lunch."

They thanked Mrs. Wurmbrand and said good-bye. Then they rang the bell of her next-door neighbor, Mrs. Ellsworth. Nora used to call her Mrs. Mind-Your-Own-Business because she never did. But recently they had become special friends.

The door opened and, looking out, Mrs. Ellsworth said, "Nora, what are you up to now?" So Nora told her the good news.

"What a lot of work for your mother, Russell," Mrs. Ellsworth said and sighed. "You must be a good boy and help her when she comes home," she said as she closed her door.

Even though they had been talking about his new sister all this time, Russell had not said a single word. He usually was quiet, and the children were used to it. But now, at the mention of his mother, he began to cry.

Nora noticed and said, "I think it's time to eat the chocolate. It's too special a day to wait for lunch, and besides, mine is beginning to melt through the paper."

Russell wiped his eyes on his sleeve and opened his candy.

"Russell!" exclaimed Nora. "We forgot to tell Henry!" Henry was the doorman, who knew everything and everybody in the building. But for once Nora knew something before he did.

They went downstairs and gave the good news to Henry.

"It's a new neighbor for you, Nora," he said, grinning and patting the top of Russell's head.

Suddenly Nora said, "Russell, guess what!" As usual she answered herself. "Now you are a big brother to baby Elisa the way I am a big sister to Teddy. Teddy is only a little brother. Isn't that funny?"

"How can I be a little brother if I am older than Russell?" asked Teddy. "It isn't fair."

"That's just the way it is," said Nora. "And when baby Elisa comes home, I'll teach her how to play with us because I'm the oldest child in this building. We can play lots of new games now that there are four of us, and we'll all have fun together."

Russell smiled as he licked the chocolate off his fingers.

MOVING CO.

More New Neighbors

From time to time an immense van would pull up in front of the building where Nora lived. The presence of the van meant that someone was either moving in or out of the house. Nora loved to watch the strong men carrying the furniture. Imagine a truck big enough to hold all the furniture from four or five rooms. The truck was big enough to live in! It was sad when someone moved away because then Nora was losing friends. But the arrival of new people was always exciting.

Now, however, the newest person to arrive was Russell's baby sister, Elisa. Nora liked her very much, but she had not done much growing yet. Nora couldn't remember when she or Teddy had been babies. She hadn't remembered that growing took so long. Whenever Nora saw her, Elisa was either sleeping or crying. Obviously it would be a long, long time before they could play together, and that was a big disappointment.

So Nora kept hoping that an already grown girl, just her size, would move into an empty apartment. Her wish would have to happen sometime. She just knew it.

One sunny Saturday in March, a new family did move into the building. Nora and Teddy, standing on the curb and peering into the truck, tried to count how many beds there were. But it was dark inside, and all the pieces of furniture were piled on top of each other. They fitted together like the three-dimensional puzzle that Teddy had gotten for his last birthday.

Nora and Teddy kept watching for a clue. Did the new tenants have children? All families have tables and chairs and chests of drawers. There was a sofa, two armchairs, and a desk. Just when it looked as if there were no clues for them at all, one of the movers emerged from the truck carrying a big carton. On one side of it someone had written the word *Toys*. Nora spelled it out for Teddy because he couldn't read yet.

"Grown-ups don't play with toys!" she said with delight. There had to be a child. And then, from the rear of the truck, one of the movers carried out a tiny, doll-sized rocking chair. That was what Nora had been waiting for. It was the absolute proof that the new family had a child and the child was a girl.

Nora wondered what she looked like and what she was named. She was certain that this girl was the special best friend she had been waiting for.

Nora and Teddy looked around them. The movers were closing up the now-empty truck, but there was no sign of the new tenants. Perhaps they were already

upstairs in their new home. The new people would be living in apartment 4E. Nora and Teddy lived in 7E, exactly three floors above.

Nora couldn't wait to introduce herself to the new neighbors. But Mommy felt they should be given a little time to move their furniture about and unpack their boxes. So not until eleven-thirty the next morning did Nora go with her mother and Teddy to greet the new people. They rang the doorbell and waited.

The door was opened by a tall man with glasses. Mommy explained that they were neighbors and welcomed him to the building. As they stood at the doorway, the man was joined by a woman. He said, "This is my wife, Mrs. Eastman. I'm Mr. Eastman."

"Won't you come in?" invited Mrs. Eastman.

Nora looked about for the girl she knew would be there. It was strange to walk into an apartment that looked exactly like her own and yet was different at the same time. The Eastmans' sofa was facing in the opposite direction from the one in Nora's living room, but the kitchen was in the same place and looked identical except for the curtains.

"How old are you?" Mrs. Eastman asked Nora. "You are probably the same age as Gene."

Nora heard the name and smiled. She was right. There was a girl: Jean. There was a girl named Jean in her class at school too.

"I'm seven years old," said Nora proudly.

She was about to ask where Jean was when she heard the toilet in the bathroom down the hall being flushed. Then two things happened almost at once. Nora noticed the little tiny rocking chair in a corner of the living room with an old-fashioned-looking doll sitting in it. And at the same moment a *boy* came walking into the room. He was tall and wore glasses and looked very much like Mr. Eastman. Nora wondered if he was Jean's brother.

"This is our son Eugene Spencer," said Mrs. Eastman. "Gene was just eight years old."

This was Jean! Nora was stunned into silence. Gene was a boy. She could not believe it, and yet there he was standing right in front of her.

Mrs. Eastman said that she was having

a problem with the stove, and the three adults walked off toward the kitchen. Nora stood looking at this new boy. She remembered that his mother said that he was eight years old. She herself had been seven for only a short while and was going to remain seven for quite a long time. When she was playing with Teddy and Russell, seven seemed very old and important. But suddenly seven didn't seem very old. This was not the way Nora had imagined things at all.

"Why do you have two names?" she asked Eugene Spencer.

"One for each of my grandfathers," Eugene said proudly. "One is named Spencer and the other is named Eugene, and we didn't want to hurt their feelings."

Nora had only one grandfather. Not

counting her last name, she had only one name, too.

"I have two names," said Teddy, beaming. "Teddy and Theodore."

"They're both the same," said Nora. "Teddy is just a short way of saying Theodore. It's not your real name. It's a nickname."

"My nickname is Gene," said Eugene Spencer, "but most people call me Eugene Spencer."

Eugene Spencer had everything: two grandfathers, two real names, *and* a nickname. Nora began to feel angry.

"If you're a boy," she asked, "why do you have a doll and a doll's chair?"

"That doll is an antique. It's very valuable and nobody plays with it," said Eugene Spencer. "It's just for looking at,

so don't you touch it. It belonged to my great-grandmother when she was a little girl."

"Do you have a great-grandmother too?" asked Nora. This awful boy seemed to have everything. She didn't have to look further in the apartment to know that he had his own bedroom down the hall.

"No, she died before I was born. She'd be over one hundred years old if she was still alive. And this doll is one hundred years old. That's why it's an antique," he explained importantly.

"Do you have a fairy godmother?" asked Teddy.

"Don't be silly," said Eugene Spencer. "Nobody has a fairy godmother, except in silly stories."

"Stories aren't silly," retorted Nora.

"And Teddy and I have a pretend fairy godmother. Her name is Mrs. Ellsworth, and she lives right here in this building. Sometimes she stays with us when our parents go out in the evening, and then we play make-believe magic."

"Aren't there any boys in this building?" asked Eugene Spencer. "In my old building we had twin brothers, just my age."

"I am a boy," said Teddy. "And Russell is a boy, too. He has a new baby sister, but she's too little to play yet."

"How old is Russell?" asked Eugene Spencer, looking interested.

"Four," said Nora.

"He's a baby. I don't play with babies."

"He's not a baby. He's our friend," said Nora. "We have lots of friends in this building. There's Mrs. Wurmbrand. We call her Mrs. W. She's like an extra grand-mother to us." Nora thought for a minute. "How many grandmothers do you have?"

"Two," said Eugene Spencer.

"Well, counting Mrs. Wurmbrand, Teddy and I have three grandmothers. I don't think Mrs. Wurmbrand would be a grandmother for you. She would probably think that *you* are a baby. She is almost eighty-six years old."

"I'm older than you," said Eugene Spencer. "Besides, I don't need any more grandmothers."

He was quiet for a minute, and then he said, "Don't you want to see my room?"

Nora wanted to say no, but she was curious in spite of herself. So she and Teddy followed him down the hallway. His room was the one that Mommy and

Daddy shared upstairs. There was a bunk bed along one wall. Eugene Spencer seemed to have two of everything.

"Who sleeps in the other part of your bed?" Nora asked.

"No one," Eugene Spencer said. "Sometimes I sleep on top and sometimes I sleep on the bottom, whichever I feel like."

For some time Nora had been wishing for a room all to herself. But now she said, "It sounds lonely to me. Teddy and I can talk to each other in the nighttime."

Mommy called to the children. It was time for them to go back to their own apartment. "We just wanted to welcome you," she said to the Eastmans. "I'm sure you will like living here very much."

Nora didn't care if they liked it here or not. In fact, if they didn't like it perhaps they would move again, and the girl she had been waiting for would come. She didn't like Eugene Spencer one bit. He was a show-off, just because he was older than she was and had two names.

When they returned to their apartment, Nora said to her mother, "I wish I had two names."

"Nora is such a lovely name that Daddy and I didn't think you needed another," her mother answered.

"Then call me Nora-Nora," said Nora.

"Sometimes I do," said Mommy.

Sure enough, in the evening when it was time for Nora's bath her mother had to call, "Nora-Nora! The water is ready now." And again when it grew late she had to say, "Nora-Nora! It's time for bed."

But in the afternoon when she asked,

"Do you want some milk and cookies, Nora?" she only had to say the name once.

Before they fell asleep in their beds that night, Teddy said, "Nora, guess what! Now that Eugene Spencer lives here, you're not the oldest child in the building anymore."

"So what!" said Nora. "It doesn't matter at all."

But it did. To Nora it mattered a whole lot.

Lying

"I hate rain!" said Nora in an angry voice.

Earlier in the week Mommy had promised Nora and Teddy that they would all go to the zoo on Saturday. But now that it was Saturday, it was raining and so they had to stay home.

"You lied to me," said Nora, pouting. She was very disappointed.

"No," said Mommy. "The weatherman predicted a warm and sunny day. I really thought we would go to the zoo. And we will sometime soon on another day."

"Then the weatherman lied," Nora said accusingly.

"No. He made a mistake," explained Mommy. "Everyone makes a mistake sometimes."

"The weatherman seems to make more than his share," commented Daddy, buttoning his coat and taking his umbrella. Even though it was Saturday, Daddy had to go to his office.

Nora was still unhappy, but she cheered up when Mommy said she could phone her classmate Sharon and invite her over to play. But Sharon was going to her cousin's birthday party. Russell had a cold.

Elisa was still too small to play.

"There's nothing to do," complained Nora.

"Maybe Eugene would like to come and play," Mommy suggested.

"Eugene Spencer thinks he's so smart just because he's eight years old," grumbled Nora. "And he only likes to play with boys."

Mommy ignored Nora's remarks and went to the telephone. She spoke to Mrs. Eastman. "Nora would like Eugene to come and play," she said.

"That was a lie," said Nora, when Mommy got off the phone. "I don't care if he wants to come or not. I don't like him at all."

"Sometimes," said Mommy, "a person says something that they don't really mean to make another person feel good. Do you remember when Anita got her hair cut, and then she came to ask me if I liked it?"

Anita used to have long hair, but one day she got it cut very short and curly, and now she looked like a different person.

"If I had told Anita that I didn't like her haircut, she would have been very sad. So I made up a little lie, and I told her that she looked lovely. That made her smile, and when Anita smiles she is very pretty no matter how she wears her hair," Mommy explained.

The doorbell rang, and there was no time for Nora to think of an answer to what her mother had said. Eugene Spencer was standing at the door.

"I'm going to start fixing some lunch," said Mommy. "How about grilled-cheese sandwiches?" All three children agreed.

"Could we have soda to drink?" asked Nora. If they had gone to the zoo they would have had hot dogs *and* soda.

Mommy thought for a moment. "Yes, I have a bottle of soda in the cupboard. I'll get out ice cubes, and you may share it." Mommy bent down and looked in the cupboard. She took out a bottle of ketchup and a box of cereal and a box of crackers and a can of coffee. She reached around in the cupboard picking out more and more of the stored groceries. There was no bottle of soda.

"I'm sorry," she said apologetically. "I guess we used up that bottle of ginger ale. I can't seem to find it."

"That's OK," said Eugene Spencer. "I can have soda at home tonight."

"I'll drink milk," said Teddy agreeably.

Nora did not feel agreeable in the least. "You lied to me," she told her mother.

"I made a mistake," said Mommy. "Everyone makes a mistake sometimes. Sometimes even twice in one day."

After lunch Eugene Spencer looked at the toys in Nora and Teddy's room. "I hate rain," he said. "There's nothing to do."

Although she had felt the same way a minute before, Nora was also feeling very contrary. She would not give Eugene Spencer the satisfaction of agreeing with him.

"There are one hundred things to do if you use your head," she said with superiority.

"Like what?" demanded Eugene Spencer.

"We could play *Wizard of Oz*. I'll be Dorothy, and Teddy can be Toto, and you could be the Wizard. Or we could be astronauts on the moon and explore it. Or we could build card houses. I just learned how from my grandmother. Or. . . ."

"No," said Eugene Spencer. "Those sound like baby games. Let's watch TV."

"I don't waste my time watching TV all day long," said Nora, who knew her mother wouldn't let her anyhow.

"Then let's ride up and down in the elevator," said Eugene Spencer.

"Where would we go?" asked Teddy, who had been listening to this discussion with interest.

"Just up and down. We could play your astronaut game in the elevator, going up and down in a space capsule."

Nora was astounded by this suggestion. "An elevator is not a toy," she said loftily. She was repeating the words of her parents whenever she and Teddy argued about whose turn it was to push the buttons.

"See? I told you there was nothing to do," complained Eugene Spencer.

Nora didn't answer. She took her deck of cards and began balancing two against each other. It was hard work, but she succeeded in making a simple house. Then she made another and another. The telephone rang, but instead of running with Teddy to try and answer it first, she kept on balancing the cards. She already had five delicate houses when Mommy came to the doorway of the bedroom.

"Eugene," she said, "your mother is on the phone. She's going out on some errands. Do you want to stay here and play or go with her?"

"I guess I'll go," said Eugene Spencer. "There's nothing special to do here." As he walked from the room he kicked out his feet, knocking down the first card house. All of the others tumbled after.

Mommy closed the apartment door behind Eugene as he left.

"I hate Eugene Spencer. I hate him," said Nora.

"I don't think he meant to knock your houses down," consoled Mommy, who had seen what happened. "I'm sure it was an accident."

"He did it on purpose," said Nora. "And I hate him."

"It isn't nice to say things like that," said Mommy.

"It's the truth," said Nora. "The absolute truth. I don't tell lies."

Under the Weather

On Monday Nora woke with an itch on her nose.

"What a funny place for a mosquito bite," she said, as she scratched it. There was another red welt on her cheek and one on her neck.

Mommy took a look and suddenly remembered a note that had come in the mail on Friday, informing her of what Nora had been exposed to at school.

"Nora," said Mommy, "don't bother to get dressed this morning. You have chicken pox. You won't be going anywhere."

"I couldn't have caught Jeffrey's chicken pox," Nora protested. "I don't even sit near him."

"Chicken pox is highly contagious," said Mommy. "Even if you only go up in the elevator with someone incubating chicken pox, you'll come down with it too."

"Chicken pox, close the box," sang Teddy. Whoever heard of a sickness with such a funny name?

"Chicken pox, dirty socks," said Daddy.

"It's not funny!" Nora pouted. "I don't

feel sick. I want to go to school, or else I'll miss the class trip." Today was the day her class was going to the bakery to see how bagels were made. Nora scratched her cheek.

Mommy grabbed Nora's hand. "Don't scratch," she said.

"Chicken pox, stones and rocks," Teddy called out. Mommy lifted Teddy onto her lap and pulled down his pajamas. There were no welts on his stomach or back.

"Sooner or later you'll get it too," she said with a sigh. "I wonder how long this will last."

"Cheer up," said Daddy. "Chicken pox is practically the only old-fashioned sickness left. Nowadays you don't get measles or whooping cough or—"

"Whooping cough, whooping cough," Teddy roared. He liked the sound of that one too.

"So long, Spots," Daddy called to Nora, leaving for his office. "I'll see you tonight."

"Chicken pox, close the locks," Teddy sang, as Daddy shut the door behind him.

"Come on, Nora," said Mommy. "What do you want for breakfast?"

"Chicken!" shouted Teddy. "When you have chicken pox you can only eat chicken and drink chicken soup!"

"Then I'd rather get roast-beef pox," grumbled Nora.

"Or chocolate pox," shouted Teddy.

"Or cookie pox," and Mommy laughed.

It was a funny sickness, for Nora didn't feel the least bit ill. She stayed home and played with her games and with Teddy, since their mother said there was no point in trying to separate the children now.

Mommy spent most of the morning on the telephone. She phoned the doctor, who just said to keep Nora comfortable and him posted. She called Russell's mother and warned her that he would probably succumb to the chicken pox before long.

"Could Elisa get chicken pox, too?" asked Nora.

"I hope not," said Mommy.

She phoned Mrs. Eastman and asked if Eugene Spencer had ever had chicken pox. He hadn't.

"Good!" shouted Nora when she heard. "I hope he gets chicken pox, turkey-lurkey pox, and goosey-loosey pox."

"That isn't very nice, Nora," said Mommy.

Nora knew it wasn't nice, and she didn't care. Since Eugene Spencer did everything in twos, she hoped he would have twice as many spots and twice as many itches when he got the pox.

Nora's mother called Grandma and Grandpa and told them the news. Grandpa spoke to Nora on the phone. "I hear you are under the weather," he said. "I'll give you a penny for every spot you get," he promised. "But you mustn't scratch them." Nora went into the bathroom where there was a full-length mirror and tried to discover if there were any more spots. No luck, just the same three old ones.

"There will be more before there are

less," Mommy reassured her. "Chicken soup for lunch," she told Nora.

The afternoon passed slowly.

Mommy refused to permit Nora to sit and watch TV, and Nora insisted that she wasn't tired enough for a nap. For a sick girl she had lots of energy. By the time Daddy came home, Nora had painted red chicken-pox spots all over her dolls with a marker, and she had played with every toy and game that she owned. Only when it was time to put them away did she decide that she felt under the weather and had better lie down on her bed. From there she watched Teddy and Mommy clean up.

The next morning and the morning afterward Nora awoke with the same three itches but no new ones at all. Mommy

searched her scalp and her back, places Nora couldn't check. There was nothing to be seen except hair and clear skin.

"This is the mildest case of chicken pox on record," marveled Mommy.

Now that Nora had resigned herself to staying home from school, she was having fun. For three days she had been receiving special invalid care: pancakes for breakfast, games and games of Chinese checkers, and both parents took turns reading aloud. Mommy read all of *Stuart Little,* and Daddy read from a copy of the *Red Fairy Book* that had been his when he was a boy.

"The best thing about chicken pox," said Daddy, "is that you can only get it once."

"Why do people get colds over and

over?" wondered Nora.

"How about turkey pox?" asked Teddy.

Thursday morning, the fourth day of the chicken pox, Mommy phoned Dr. Clive. "I think she's better," she said. "Can she return to school?" The doctor said that no one ever recovered from chicken pox so quickly, but he agreed to take a look at Nora if Mommy brought her to his office at noon. They took a taxi and went right in so that no one would catch Nora's germs.

Doctor Clive examined the fading spots and burst out laughing.

"Nora, you are a wonder!" he said.

"What is so funny about my pox?" asked Nora.

"These aren't chicken pox. You have a case of early mosquito bites!"

"In April?" gasped Mommy.

"It's a good trick," agreed the doctor. "It only takes a warm day to get the mosquitoes out. I've known people to get mosquito bites in January." He wrote out a note so that Nora could return to school the next day. Then he gave the note to her mother and a yellow lollipop to Nora.

They took a subway home.

"Why don't we take another taxi?" asked Nora.

"Because you're not sick," said Mommy.

Two weeks later Nora had chicken pox again. Her case would have been a medical first, except the second time was still the first. "I'm getting like Eugene Spencer," grumbled Nora. "Doing things in twos."

The real chicken pox was not nearly as

much fun as the fake chicken pox. Nora's face and chest and back were covered with tiny blisters that itched and irritated her. Furthermore, she had a runny nose and even a little fever.

Old Mrs. Wurmbrand tried to cheer Nora by bringing her a chocolate bar and a bright red apple.

Mrs. Ellsworth, who as usual didn't want to mind her own business, came to see Nora too. "Don't scratch," she said, "or you'll have scars forever."

"Cheer up," said Daddy. "This is really the last time you'll have chicken pox."

And it was, for Nora. But two weeks later Teddy got his chicken pox. Luckily neither Russell nor baby Elisa got it. But last of all, and best of all, as far as Nora was concerned, Eugene Spencer got chicken pox too. "He got the chicken-chicken pox-pox," said Nora.

But when Mommy insisted, she made him a get-well card.

Gum Day

Everyone Nora and Teddy knew chewed gum. Well, perhaps not everyone. Mrs. Wurmbrand didn't, and Grandma and Grandpa didn't, and Mommy and Daddy didn't. Russell and Elisa didn't. They were both too young. But everyone else did. All the children in Nora's first-grade class chewed gum. The mailman chewed, and the cashier at the check-out counter at the supermarket chewed. Eugene Spencer chewed. Almost everyone.

"It's not a nice habit," said Mommy.

"It's bad for your teeth," said Daddy.

But Nora was not convinced. She begged so often and came home with gifts of gum from her classmates so frequently that finally her parents decided on a compromise.

Wednesday was Gum Day.

That meant that Nora was on her honor not to put a single piece of gum inside her mouth on any day of the week except Wednesday. But on Wednesday she could chew all she wanted.

"It really isn't fair," Nora complained. "Mrs. Kessler won't let us chew in class, so I lose a lot of chewing time."

"If you did nothing but chew gum from the moment you woke up until the moment you went to bed, your jaws would ache terribly," comforted Mommy. "Enjoy the time you have."

And it was true. Once, when school was closed on a Wednesday, Nora put gum in her mouth as soon as she finished breakfast and by lunchtime she was worn out with chewing. But most weeks she couldn't get enough.

Nora saved her pennies and collected gum balls from the machine in the supermarket. She traded the cookies in her lunch box with her classmates for wrapped sticks of gum. Nora liked mint-flavored gums and fruit-flavored gums. Best of all, she loved the sweet, sweet taste of pink bubble gum. Yet, much as she loved the flavor, Nora didn't know how to blow bubbles.

She watched with fascination as Maggie made enormous bubbles while pushing the keys on the cash register in the supermarket. Imagine being able to do two such difficult things at one time.

This Wednesday afternoon, even though she was chewing on a piece of her precious gum, Nora was in a bad mood. Mommy had promised Eugene Spencer's mother that he could stay with Nora and Teddy after school. Mrs. Eastman was applying to go back to school, and she had to go for an interview. Nora hadn't known that even grown-ups sometimes went to school, and she didn't want to spend the afternoon with that awful Eugene Spencer.

"Give Eugene a piece of gum, if he wants one," Mommy instructed Nora. Of course Eugene Spencer wanted a piece, and a minute later he produced an enormous pink bubble.

"Let's have a contest and see who can make the biggest bubbles," suggested Eugene Spencer. "I usually chew two pieces at once," he said. "Then I can make really gigantic bubbles."

"I don't want to," said Nora. She also didn't want Eugene Spencer to know that she couldn't make bubbles at all.

"What's the matter? Can't you do it?" guessed Eugene. "You must be retarded!"

He chewed his gum thoughtfully. "Watch me. It's very easy," he said.

"Let's see," said Teddy. He wasn't into chewing gum yet. He still was big on lollipops, which he got at the barbershop and from various people. Lollipops were allowed any day of the week, and although they seemed rather babyish on Wednesdays, Nora was known to enjoy them on other days.

Eugene pressed the gum against the inside of his front teeth and pursed his lips. He blew a little air into the gum and it began to expand, forming the desired bubble. It looked so easy that Nora forgot her reluctance to exhibit her ignorance and began to try. Unfortunately, when she tried to push the gum against her teeth with her tongue, she accidentally spit it onto the floor.

"Just pick it up and put it back in your mouth," said Eugene Spencer.

The second time the gum fell Mommy

walked into the room.

"Oh, no!" she said. "If gum falls on the floor, it goes right into the garbage." They had the same rule for cookies, candy, raisins, and other eatable things that fell on the ground.

"Why can't you wash it with soap?" asked Teddy.

When it was time for Eugene Spencer to go home, Nora had still not mastered the art of bubble-gum blowing. He had been more understanding of Nora when Teddy explained that she was permitted to chew gum only on Wednesdays. "No wonder you haven't learned yet," he said. "For me, every day is gum day."

After supper, when Nora was bathed and in her pajamas but still hadn't brushed her teeth for the night, she took her last piece of gum for the week and unwrapped it. This would be her last chance till next Wednesday. She chewed the gum slowly, enjoying the sugary taste that always disappeared too quickly. When the gum seemed smooth against her tongue, she went through the routines that Eugene Spencer had taught her.

Daddy walked into the bedroom and stood watching. "Cows chew their cud," he said. "I wonder if they think it's gum?"

"If they made bubbles," said Nora, "maybe milk would taste more like soda."

She stopped talking and tried again. Suddenly the gum pressed against her teeth began to give and a small bubble formed from it. There was a mirror on the closet door, and Nora ran to look. She could hardly believe her eyes. She couldn't talk because the gum with its bubble would fall out, so she ran to the living room to show her mother and Teddy.

"Nora. You did it!" Teddy shouted. Even Mommy seemed amused.

"Do it again," said Teddy.

Nora was afraid. Suppose she couldn't do it a second time. Reluctantly she chewed down on her bubble and tried again. It worked! A new little bubble formed and then broke with a small pop.

"It's like a little balloon," said Teddy, fascinated by the process. This was certainly more exciting than lollipops.

Nora blew six more bubbles before Mommy told her to spit out the gum and brush her teeth. It was bedtime.

"Suppose I forget how to do it before next Wednesday," she mourned.

"You won't," promised Daddy.

"Could I just chew one piece of gum tomorrow to show Eugene Spencer?"

"No," said Daddy. "You know the rule. No chewing except on Wednesday!"

"Then I must go downstairs and show Eugene Spencer right now. I'll put on my bathrobe, and it will only take a minute," Nora insisted.

"He's probably in bed already," said Mommy.

"He wouldn't be in bed," said Nora. "He's older so he can stay up much later than I can. He told me that."

"I'll phone his mother and see if it's all right while you're getting your bathrobe," said Mommy, giving in.

A minute later Nora was in the elevator on her way to see Eugene Spencer. It was the first time she had ever been in the elevator in her pajamas, but that was the nice thing about having friends in your own building. You didn't need a coat to go visiting.

As she rang the bell of apartment 4E, Nora chewed her gum into position. She began a bubble just as the door opened. There stood Mrs. Eastman and Eugene Spencer together. Eugene Spencer was wearing his pajamas, too. They watched as Nora's bubble grew larger and larger.

"Wow, that's pretty good," said Eugene Spencer.

The bubble broke with a loud pop.

"Neat-o," said Eugene Spencer. "You're a good bubble-gum blower."

"You're a good bubble-gum teacher," admitted Nora.

Mrs. Eastman interrupted. "Nora, I promised your mother to send you home immediately, and besides, it's Eugene Spencer's bedtime."

"Let's make more bubbles tomorrow," said Eugene Spencer. "We can have our contest now."

"I can't," said Nora. "Not till next Gum Day."

"Well, we could play together anyhow," suggested Eugene.

"OK," agreed Nora, blowing her very last bubble of the evening. As she went into the elevator it gave a good-bye pop to Eugene Spencer.

Singing in the Rain

It was the last day of June, and school was over until the fall. Nora had finished first grade, and in September she would be in second grade like Eugene Spencer. The only trouble was that Eugene Spencer had finished second grade and he would be entering third grade. Nora would never catch up.

Oh, well, thought Nora. I'll always be ahead of Teddy. In the fall Teddy would start kindergarten.

Eugene Spencer's mother had begun attending school, and she even had classes in the summertime. So Eugene Spencer had come to the park with Teddy and Nora. Mommy sat nearby on a park bench speaking to Mrs. Michaels, who was rocking a carriage with baby Elisa. Nora and Eugene Spencer were riding up and down on the seesaw while Teddy was busy digging in the sandbox with Russell.

Because it was a very hot day, Mommy and Mrs. Michaels had given their permission for the children to play barefoot. Nora had removed her sandals, and Teddy and Eugene Spencer and

Russell their sneakers and socks. It really was summer when you could feel the warm ground under your bare feet.

From time to time Nora would stop playing and run and peek into the baby carriage. Elisa had started growing at last. She still had no teeth or hair and couldn't talk, but she did appear bigger than when she first came home from the hospital. Mrs. Michaels said that soon she would be able to sit up by herself. But it would be a long while before she could join the other children at their games. Sometimes Mrs. Michaels let Nora push the carriage gently back and forth. She gave all the children turns: Russell first, because he was the big brother, then Nora and Teddy. Even Eugene Spencer asked to have a turn.

Since he didn't have any brother or sister, they all had to share theirs with him.

Now Mrs. Michaels called to Russell. "It looks to me as if it is going to rain. And I want to pick up some fruit before we go home."

Russell reluctantly left the sandbox. "Good-bye," called Teddy, continuing to fill his pail as the Michaels left the park.

"Teddy, Nora, Eugene," called Mommy. "It's getting dark. We ought to go too before we get caught in the rain."

"Just another minute," called Nora. "Eugene and I are going to see who can go the highest on the swings." She jumped off the seesaw, and Eugene Spencer landed with a thump. He ran after Nora toward the swings.

Teddy climbed out of the sandbox.

His mother said, "Teddy, you should get a prize for being the dirtiest boy in the park." In addition to sand, there was chocolate ice cream on his face and brown stains on his chest. From his toenails to his scalp, he was a grubby, sandy mess.

"You'll have to get right into the bathtub, even before supper," said his mother.

She gathered up her canvas bag, which she always carried to the park. It held her library book, tissues, a box of Band-Aids, and a box of pretzels. Sometimes its contents included a picnic lunch. Today it also held a small bag of grocery items that they had stopped for on the way to the park: three bars of soap, a can of mushroom soup, and two cans of tuna fish.

"I think I felt a drop of rain," said Mommy.

Teddy couldn't find his socks. He had pulled them off so eagerly that he hadn't even bothered to put them inside his sneakers. "It's raining!" he said, feeling a drop hit the back of his neck.

"Nora-Nora," Mommy called again.

The two children jumped from the swings. All about them mothers were putting toddlers into strollers and pulling the hoods up on baby carriages.

"Hurry," called Mommy, as the rain began to fall in earnest. "Don't bother with your shoes," she said. "Let's just make a run for it." She grabbed the sneakers and sandals from under the park bench and threw them into her canvas bag.

"Come. Let's run home," she said.

The three children began to run. But the rough sidewalk made running with bare feet difficult. The rain came down harder than before.

"Hurry," said Mommy, rushing ahead, "or we will get all wet!"

The warm rain felt good on Nora's skin.

"Stop! Why are we running?" Nora asked. "We're already wet."

Mommy stopped to catch her breath. Her wet hair hung from her head just as it did when she had a shampoo. Her clothes were wet and stuck to her skin. Nora and Teddy and Eugene were thoroughly wet, too. The rain was pouring down, but there was no thunder or lightning.

"I can't get *more* wet," said Nora.

"Me too," said Teddy. "I am as wet as in the bath."

"Too bad we haven't any soap or towels. You could take a bath," Mommy said with a laugh.

"We have soap," Nora remembered, and she dug into the wet canvas bag. In a moment she and Teddy had torn the wrapping from two of the soap bars. They gave a bar to Eugene, too. Then they started scrubbing themselves with more vigor than they ever used in the tub at home.

Mommy stood laughing so hard that tears came out of her eyes and mixed with the raindrops on her face.

"This is the best shower I ever took," said Teddy, rubbing the dirt from his

knees. He began to chant:

"Rub-a-dub-dub
Three men in a tub
And who do you think they be?"

"It's Eugene and Teddy and me," shouted Nora, delighted by her change in the old rhyme.

Even as they washed the rain began to let up.

"Oh, I think it's stopping," said Eugene Spencer with disappointment.

"These sudden, heavy rains never last very long," said Mommy. "Come. We'll go home and get some towels and dry clothing. Your mother will be worrying about you, Eugene."

They headed toward their apartment

building, but they didn't run. They walked slowly, enjoying the last drops of rain that rinsed them off. The streets had that special, good smell that they always had after a rain. There were little rainbows in the puddles on Broadway caused by oil mixing with water on the street.

"Teddy, this is the first day you have come home from the park so clean," said Mommy. "People will think you are growing up."

"No," said Teddy. "Not yet. I'll be dirty again tomorrow."

"Well," said Nora, "not if it rains on you."

"Let's hope tomorrow is a sunny day," said Mommy.

"That's OK. It doesn't matter," said Nora. "I love weather. We will have fun even if the sun isn't shining."

"Sure," agreed Eugene Spencer. "We always have fun together."

"Yes," said Nora, as she splashed in a puddle. "Rain or shine. And that's the truth!"

Johanna Hurwitz

is the author of BUSYBODY NORA, SUPERDUPER TEDDY, RIP-ROARING RUSSELL, RUSSELL AND ELISA, RUSSELL SPROUTS, and other popular books about the Riverside Kids. She has worked as a children's librarian in school and public libraries in New York City and on Long Island, and she frequently visits schools around the country to talk about books with students, teachers, librarians, and parents. Mrs. Hurwitz and her husband live in Great Neck, New York. They are the parents of two grown children.